This book belongs to

ANIMAL

Crackers

A Delectable Collection of

Pictures, Poems, and Lullabies for the Very Young

JANE DYER

Little, Brown and Company

Boston   New York   Toronto   London

TABLE

OF CONTENTS

Nursery Rhymes • 34

Playtime • 42

Lullaby and Good Night • 50

ABC, 123,

A B C D E

A K L M N

S T U V

SHAPES, COLORS

F G H I J

O P Q R

W X Y Z

1 2 3 4 5 6 7 8 9 10

ONE, TWO, BUCKLE MY SHOE

One, two,
Buckle my shoe;

Three, four,
Knock at the door;

Five, six,
Pick up sticks;

Seven, eight,
Lay them straight;

Nine, ten,
A good fat hen.

1, 2, BUCKLE MY SHOE . . .

1, 2, 3, 4, 5, 6, 7, 8, 9, 10...

ONE, TWO, THREE, FOUR, FIVE

One, two, three, four, five,
Once I caught a fish alive.

Six, seven, eight, nine, ten,
Then I let it go again.

Why did you let it go?
Because it bit my finger so.
Which finger did it bite?
This little finger on the right.

SEVEN BLACKBIRDS IN A TREE

Seven blackbirds in a tree,
Count them and see what they be.
One for sorrow,
Two for joy,
Three for a girl,
Four for a boy;
Five for silver,
Six for gold,
Seven for a secret
That's never been told.

9

COLOR

What is pink? A rose is pink
By a fountain's brink.

What is red? A poppy's red
In its barley bed.

What is blue? The sky is blue
Where the clouds float through.

What is white? A swan is white
Sailing in the light.

What is yellow? Pears are yellow,
Rich and ripe and mellow.

What is green? The grass is green,
With small flowers between.

What is violet? Clouds are violet
In the summer twilight.

What is orange? Why, an orange,
Just an orange!

Christina Rossetti

THE END

When I was One,
I had just begun.

When I was Two,
I was nearly new.

When I was Three,
I was hardly Me.

When I was Four,
I was not much more.

When I was Five,
I was just alive.

But now I am Six, I'm as clever as clever.
So I think I'll be Six now for ever and ever.

A. A. Milne

A WAS AN APPLE

A APPLE PIE

A	was an Apple Pie
B	Bit it
C	Cut it
D	Dealt it
E	Eat it
F	Fought for it
G	Got it
H	Had it
I	Inspected it
J	Jumped for it
K	Knelt for it
L	Longed for it
M	Mourned for it
N	Nodded at it
O	Opened it
P	Peeped at it
Q	Quartered it
R	Ran for it
S	Sang for it
T	Took it
U	Upset it
V	Viewed it
W	Wanted it

X, Y, and Z

All had a large slice and went off to bed.

PIE...

WINTER

SPRING

SUMMER

FALL

THE MONTHS OF THE YEAR

January brings the snow,
Makes our feet and fingers glow.

February brings the rain,
Thaws the frozen lake again.

March brings breezes loud and shrill,
Stirs the dancing daffodil.

April brings the primrose sweet,
Scatters daisies at our feet.

May brings flocks of pretty lambs,
Skipping by their fleecy dams.

June brings tulips, lilies, roses,
Fills the children's hands with posies.

Hot July brings cooling showers,
Apricots, and gillyflowers.

August brings the sheaves of corn,
Then the harvest home is borne.

Clear September brings blue skies,
Goldenrod, and apple pies.

Fresh October brings the pheasant;
Then to gather nuts is pleasant.

Dull November brings the blast,
Makes the leaves go whirling fast.

Chill December brings the sleet,
Blazing fire, and Christmas treat.

MONDAY'S CHILD

Monday's child is fair of face,
Tuesday's child is full of grace,

Wednesday's child is full of woe,
Thursday's child has far to go,

Friday's child is loving and giving,
Saturday's child works hard for a living,

But the child that is born on Sunday
Is bonny and blithe and good and gay.

SNEEZE ON MONDAY

Sneeze on Monday, sneeze for danger;
Sneeze on Tuesday, kiss a stranger;
Sneeze on Wednesday, receive a letter;
Sneeze on Thursday, something better;
Sneeze on Friday, expect sorrow;
Sneeze on Saturday, joy tomorrow.

HOW MANY DAYS HAS MY BABY TO PLAY?

How many days has my baby to play?
Saturday, Sunday, Monday —
Tuesday, Wednesday, Thursday, Friday,
Saturday, Sunday, Monday.

TOMMY SNOOKS

As Tommy Snooks and Bessy Brooks
Were walking out one Sunday,
Said Tommy Snooks to Bessy Brooks,
"Tomorrow will be Monday."

FOOD,

FOOD, AND

FOOD,

MORE FOOD

LADIES AND GENTLEMEN

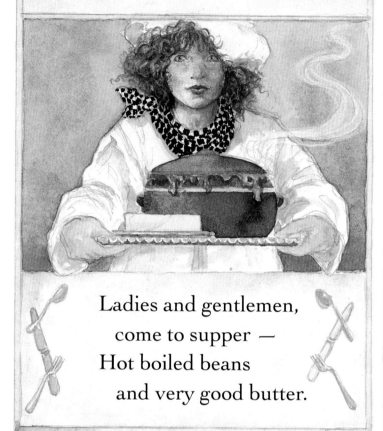

Ladies and gentlemen,
come to supper —
Hot boiled beans
and very good butter.

PEASE PORRIDGE HOT

Pease porridge hot,
Pease porridge cold,
Pease porridge in the pot
Nine days old.

Some like it hot,
Some like it cold,
Some like it in the pot
Nine days old.

HOT CROSS BUNS

Hot cross buns!
Hot cross buns!
One a penny, two a penny,
Hot cross buns!

Hot cross buns!
Hot cross buns!
If you have no daughters,
Give them to your sons.

I EAT MY PEAS WITH HONEY

I eat my peas with honey;
I've done it all my life.
It makes the peas taste funny,
But it keeps them on the knife.

ANIMAL CRACKERS

Animal crackers, and cocoa to drink,
That is the finest of suppers, I think;
When I'm grown up and can have what I please,
I think I shall always insist upon these.

Christopher Morley

IF ALL THE WORLD WERE APPLE PIE

IF ALL THE WORLD WERE APPLE PIE

If all the world were apple pie,
And all the sea were ink,
And all the trees were bread and cheese,
What would we have to drink?

COFFEE AND TEA

My sister, Molly, and I fell out,
And what do you think it was about?
She loved coffee and I loved tea,
And that was the reason we couldn't agree.

POLLY, PUT THE KETTLE ON

Polly, put the kettle on,
Polly, put the kettle on,
Polly, put the kettle on —
We'll all have tea.

Sukey, take it off again,
Sukey, take it off again,
Sukey, take it off again —
They've all gone away.

WASH THE DISHES

Wash the dishes, wipe the dishes,
Ring the bell for tea;
Three good wishes, three good kisses,
I will give to thee.

BAA, BAA

ANIMALS.

COCK-A-DOODLE-DOO

NEIGH, NEIGH

OINK, OINK

BOW-WOW

BUCK, BUCK

QUACK, QUACK

ANIMALS

HEE-HAW

MEW, MEW

MOO, MOO

27

COCK-A-DOODLE-DOO

Cock-a-doodle-doo!
My dame has lost her shoe;
My master's lost his fiddling stick
And doesn't know what to do!

BOW-WOW-WOW!

Bow-wow-wow!
Whose dog art thou?
Little Tommy Tinker's dog,
Bow-wow-wow!

BAA, BAA, BLACK SHEEP

Baa, baa, black sheep,
Have you any wool?
Yes, sir, yes, sir,
Three bags full:
One for my master,
And one for my dame,
And one for the little boy
Who lives down the lane.

OLD NOAH

Old Noah did build himself an ark;
He built one out of hickory bark;
There's one wide river to cross.

The animals went in two by two,
The elephant and the kangaroo;
There's one wide river to cross.

The animals went in three by three,
The big baboon and the chimpanzee;
There's one wide river to cross.

The animals went in four by four,
The hippopotamus blocked the door;
There's one wide river to cross!

◄ O L D ▲ N O A H ►

BOW-WOW, SAYS THE DOG

Bow-wow, says the dog;
Mew, mew, says the cat;
Grunt, grunt, goes the hog;
And squeak, goes the rat.

Chirp, chirp, says the sparrow;
Caw, caw, says the crow;
Quack, quack, says the duck;
And what cuckoos say, you know.

So, with sparrows and cuckoos,
With rats and with dogs,
With ducks and with crows,
With cats and with hogs,

A fine song I have made,
To please you, my dear;
And if it's well sung,
'Twill be charming to hear.

POEM

As the cat
climbed over
the top of

the jamcloset
first the right
forefoot

carefully
then the hind
stepped down

into the pit of
the empty
flowerpot

William Carlos Williams

THE WISE COW ENJOYS A CLOUD

"Where did you sleep last night, Wise Cow?
    Where did you lay your head?"

"I caught my horns on a rolling cloud
    and made myself a bed,

and in the morning ate it raw
    on freshly buttered bread."

Nancy Willard

THE PRAYER OF THE LITTLE DUCKS

Dear God,
        give us a flood of water.
        Let it rain tomorrow and always.
        Give us plenty of little slugs
        and other luscious things to eat.
        Protect all folk who quack
        and everyone who knows how to swim.
            Amen

Carmen Bernos de Gasztold
Translated by Rumer Godden

ALL ASLEEP

A lamb has a lambkin,
A duck has a duckling,
And I have a baby,
Good night,
Good night,
I have a baby,
Good night.

An owl has an owlet,
A pig has a suckling,
And I have a baby,
Good night,
Sleep tight,
I have a baby,
Good night.

Even a frog
Has a wee polliwog,
And I have a baby.
Star light,
Star bright,
I have a baby.
Good night.

Charlotte Pomerantz

33

NURSERY

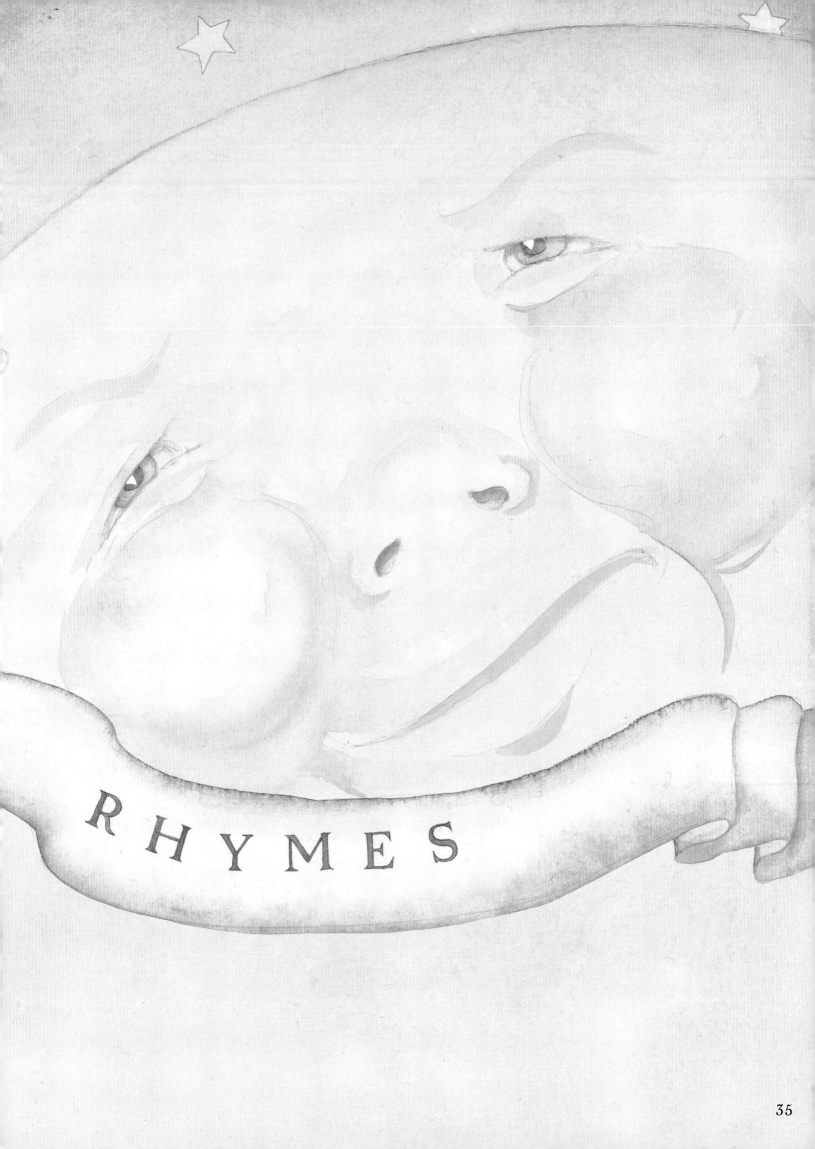

RHYMES

LITTLE JACK HORNER

Little Jack Horner
Sat in a corner,
Eating his Christmas pie;

He put in his thumb
And pulled out a plum
And said, "What a good boy am I!"

HEY, DIDDLE, DIDDLE,

HEY, DIDDLE, DIDDLE

Hey, diddle, diddle,
The cat and the fiddle,
The cow jumped over the moon;
The little dog laughed
To see such sport,
And the dish ran away with the spoon.

37

PETER PIPER

Peter Piper picked a peck of pickled pepper;
A peck of pickled pepper Peter Piper picked;
If Peter Piper picked a peck of pickled pepper,
Where's the peck of pickled pepper Peter Piper picked?

THERE WAS A LITTLE GIRL

There was a little girl, and she had a little curl
Right in the middle of her forehead;
When she was good, she was very, very good,
But when she was bad, she was horrid.

WEE WILLIE WINKIE

Wee Willie Winkie
Runs through the town,
Upstairs and downstairs
In his nightgown,
Rapping at the window,
Crying through the lock,
"Are the children in their beds,
For it's now eight o'clock!"

HUMPTY DUMPTY

Humpty Dumpty sat on a wall,
Humpty Dumpty had a great fall;
All the king's horses
And all the king's men
Couldn't put Humpty together again.

THE QUEEN OF HEARTS

The Queen of Hearts, she made some tarts
All on a summer's day;
The Knave of Hearts, he stole those tarts
And took them quite away.

DIDDLE, DIDDLE, DUMPLING

Diddle, diddle, dumpling, my son John
Went to bed with his stockings on,
One shoe off and one shoe on,
Diddle, diddle, dumpling, my son John.

LITTLE BO-PEEP

Little Bo-Peep has lost her sheep,
And can't tell where to find them;
Leave them alone, and they'll come home,
Wagging their tails behind them.

SING A SONG OF SIXPENCE

Sing a song of sixpence,
A pocketful of rye;
Four-and-twenty blackbirds
Baked in a pie.
When the pie was opened,
The birds began to sing;
Was not that a dainty dish
To set before the king?

The king was in his counting-house,
Counting out his money;
The queen was in the parlor,
Eating bread and honey;
The maid was in the garden,
Hanging out the clothes,
There came a little blackbird,
And snapped off her nose.

PLAYTIME

PAT-A-CAKE

Pat-a-cake, pat-a-cake, baker's man,
Bake me a cake as fast as you can;
Pat it and prick it, and mark it with *B*,
And put it in the oven for baby and me.

TO MARKET, TO MARKET

To market, to market, to buy a plum bun;
Home again, home again, market is done.

To market, to market, to buy a fat pig;
Home again, home again, jiggety-jig.

To market, to market, to buy a fat hog;
Home again, home again, jiggety-jog.

RIDE A COCKHORSE

Ride a cockhorse to Banbury Cross,
To see a fine lady upon a white horse;
With rings on her fingers and bells on her toes,
She shall make music wherever she goes.

RING AROUND THE ROSIE

Ring around the rosie,
A pocket full of posies,
Ashes! Ashes!
We all fall down.

THIS LITTLE PIGGY

This little piggy went to market,
This little piggy stayed at home,
This little piggy had roast beef,
This little piggy had none,
And this little piggy cried,
Wee-wee-wee,
All the way home.

I'M A LITTLE TEAPOT

I'm a little teapot, short and stout.
Here is my handle; here is my spout.
When I get all steamed up, then I shout,
"Just tip me over and pour me out."

TEDDY BEAR, TEDDY BEAR...

TEDDY BEAR, TEDDY BEAR

Teddy Bear, Teddy Bear, turn around;
Teddy Bear, Teddy Bear, touch the ground.
Teddy Bear, Teddy Bear, show your shoe;
Teddy Bear, Teddy Bear, that will do.

Teddy Bear, Teddy Bear, go up stairs;
Teddy Bear, Teddy Bear, say your prayers.
Teddy Bear, Teddy Bear, turn out the light;
Teddy Bear, Teddy Bear, say good night.

CLICKETY-CLACK

Clickety-clack,
Wheels on the track,
This is the way
They begin the attack:
Click-ety-clack,
Click-ety-clack,
Click-ety, *clack*-ety,
Click-ety
Clack.

Clickety-clack,
Over the crack,
Faster and faster
The song of the track:
Clickety-clack,
Clickety-clack,
Clickety-clackety,
Clackety
Clack.

Riding in front,
Riding in back,
Everyone hears
The song of the track:
Clickety-clack,
Clickety-clack,
Clickety, *clickety*,
Clackety
Clack.

David McCord

THE ZOO IN THE PARK

Here we go to the zoo in the park,
The zoo in the park, the zoo in the park.
Here we go to the zoo in the park,
So early in the morning.

This is the way the elephant walks,
The elephant walks, the elephant walks.
This is the way the elephant walks,
So early in the morning.

This is the way the kangaroo hops,
The kangaroo hops, the kangaroo hops.
This is the way the kangaroo hops,
So early in the morning.

This is the way the monkey jumps,
The monkey jumps, the monkey jumps.
This is the way the monkey jumps,
So early in the morning.

This is the way the birdie flies,
The birdie flies, the birdie flies.
This is the way the birdie flies,
So early in the morning.

BOOM, BOOM, BOOM

THE ORCHESTRA

Oh, we can play on the big bass drum,
And this is the music to it:
Boom, boom, boom, goes the big bass drum,
And that's the way we do it!

Oh, we can play on the violin,
And this is the music to it:
Fiddle-dee-dee, goes the violin,
And that's the way we do it.

Oh, we can play on the silver flute,
And this is the music to it:
Toot-toot-toot, goes the silver flute,
And that's the way we do it.

Oh, we can play on the big bass horn,
And this is the music to it:
Um-pah-pah, goes the big bass horn,
And that's the way we do it.

UM-PAH-PAH, UM-PAH-PAH

49

GOOD NIGHT

GOLDEN SLUMBERS

Golden slumbers kiss your eyes,
Smiles awake you when you rise.
Sleep, pretty baby, do not cry,
And I will sing a lullaby.
Rock them, rock them, lullaby.

Care is heavy, therefore sleep you,
You are care, and care must keep you.
Sleep, pretty baby, do not cry,
And I will sing a lullaby.
Rock them, rock them, lullaby.

Thomas Dekker

STAR LIGHT, STAR BRIGHT

Star light, star bright,
First star I've seen tonight,
I wish you may, I wish you might
Give me the wish I wish tonight.

THE MOON

Tonight the color
Of the moon
Is amber tea
In a silver spoon.

Kathryn Maxwell Smith

SLEEP, BABY, SLEEP
(German Lullaby)

Sleep, baby, sleep!
Thy father watches the sheep;
Thy mother is shaking the dreamland tree,
And down falls a little dream on thee:
Sleep, baby, sleep!

Sleep, baby, sleep!
The large stars are the sheep;
The wee stars are the lambs, I guess,
The fair moon is the shepherdess:
Sleep, baby, sleep!

LULLABY

Sh   sh   what do you wish
sh   sh   the windows are shuttered
sh   sh   a magical fish
swims out from the window and down to the river

lap   lap   the waters are lapping
sh   sh   the shore slips away
glide   glide   glide   with the current
sh   sh   the shadows are deeper

sleep   sleep   tomorrow is sure

Eve Merriam

SWEET AND LOW

Sweet and low, sweet and low,
Wind of the western sea,
Low, low, breathe and blow,
Wind of the western sea,
Over the rolling waters go,
Come from the dying moon, and blow,
Blow him again to me;
While my little one, while my pretty one, sleeps.

Sleep and rest, sleep and rest,
Father will come to thee soon;
Rest, rest, on mother's breast,
Father will come to thee soon.
Father will come to his babe in the nest,
Silver sails all out of the west
Under the silver moon.
Sleep, my little one, sleep, my pretty one, sleep.

Alfred, Lord Tennyson

AFRICAN LULLABY

Someone would like to have you as her child
But you are mine.
Someone would like to rear you on a costly mat
But you are mine.
Someone would like to place you on a camel blanket
But you are mine.
I have you to rear on a torn old mat,
Someone would like to have you as her child
But you are mine.

WYNKEN, BLYNKEN, AND NOD
(Dutch Lullaby)

Wynken, Blynken, and Nod one night
Sailed off in a wooden shoe —
Sailed on a river of crystal light,
Into a sea of dew.
"Where are you going, and what do you wish?"
The old moon asked the three.
"We have come to fish for the herring fish
That live in this beautiful sea:
Nets of silver and gold have we!"
    Said Wynken,
    Blynken,
    And Nod.

The old moon laughed and sang a song,
As they rocked in the wooden shoe,
And the wind that sped them all night long
Ruffled the waves of dew.
The little stars were the herring fish
That lived in that beautiful sea —
"Now cast your nets wherever you wish —
Never afeard are we;"
So cried the stars to the fishermen three:
    Wynken,
    Blynken,
    And Nod.

AND NOD

All night long their nets they threw
To the stars in the twinkling foam —
Then down from the skies came the wooden shoe,
Bringing the fishermen home;
'Twas all so pretty a sail it seemed
As if it could not be,
And some folks thought 'twas a dream they'd dreamed
Of sailing that beautiful sea —
But I shall name you the fishermen three:
    Wynken,
    Blynken,
    And Nod.

Wynken and Blynken are two little eyes,
And Nod is a little head,
And the wooden shoe that sailed the skies
Is a wee one's trundle-bed.
So shut your eyes while mother sings
Of wonderful sights that be,
And you shall see the beautiful things
As you rock in the misty sea,
Where the old shoe rocked the fishermen three:
    Wynken,
    Blynken,
    And Nod.

Eugene Field

CRADLE SONG OF THE ELEPHANTS
(Brazilian Lullaby)

The little elephant was crying
because it did not want to sleep. . .
Go to sleep, my little elephant,
the moon is going to hear you weep.

Papa elephant is near.
I hear him bellowing among the mangoes.
Go to sleep, my little elephant,
the moon will hear my little fellow. . .

Adriano del Valle
Translated by Alida Malkus

GRANDPA BEAR'S LULLABY

The night is long
But fur is deep.
You will be warm
In winter sleep.

The food is gone
But dreams are sweet
And they will be
Your winter meat.

The cave is dark
But dreams are bright
And they will serve
As winter light.

Sleep, my little cubs, sleep.

Jane Yolen

Where did you come from, baby dear?
Out of the everywhere into here.

Where did you get your eyes so blue?
Out of the sky as I came through.

What makes the light in them sparkle and spin?
Some of the starry spikes left in.

Where did you get that little tear?
I found it waiting when I got here.

What makes your forehead so smooth and high?
A soft hand stroked it as I went by.

What makes your cheek like a warm white rose?
I saw something better than anyone knows.

Whence that three-cornered smile of bliss?
Three angels gave me at once a kiss.

Where did you get this pearly ear?
God spoke, and it came out to hear.

Where did you get those arms and hands?
Love made itself into hooks and bands.

Feet, whence did you come, darling things?
From the same box as the cherubs' wings.

How did they all just come to be you?
God thought about me, and so I grew.

But how did you come to us, you dear?
God thought about you, and so I am here.

George MacDonald

FROM, BABY DEAR?

61

A VERSE FOR THE NIGHT BEFORE THE BIRTHDAY

When I have said my evening prayer,
And my clothes are folded on the chair,
And mother switches off the light,
I'll still be ___ years old tonight.
But from the very break of day,
Before the children rise and play,
Before the darkness turns to gold,
Tomorrow, I'll be ___ years old.
___ kisses when I wake,
___ candles on my cake!

M. Meyerkort

ALL TUCKED IN & ROASTY TOASTY

All tucked in & roasty toasty
Blow me a kiss good-night
Close your eyes till morning comes
Happy dreams & sleep tight

Clyde Watson

INDEX

*For my twin sister, Jean, who shared all her books
and all her meals with me from the very beginning*

Copyright © 1996 by Jane Dyer

First Edition

Acknowledgments are given as follows for permission to reprint copyrighted material:
Carmen Bernos de Gasztold: "The Prayer of the Little Ducks" from *Prayers from the Ark*, by Carmen
Bernos de Gasztold, translated by Rumer Godden. Translation copyright © 1962 by Rumer Godden.
Original copyright 1946, © 1955 by Editions de Cloitre. Used by permission of Viking Penguin, a division
of Penguin Books USA Inc. ★ **Adriano del Valle:** "Cradle Song of the Elephants," by Adriano del Valle,
translated by Alida Malkus, from *Favorite Poems Old and New*, edited by Helen Ferris. Translation copyright
© 1957 by Alida Malkus, reprinted by permission of William V. R. Malkus. ★ **David McCord:** "Clickety-
Clack" from *One at a Time*, copyright 1952 by David McCord, reprinted by permission of Little, Brown
and Company. ★ **Eve Merriam:** "Lullaby" from *Out Loud*, copyright © 1973 by Eve Merriam, reprinted by
permission of Marian Reiner. ★ **A. A. Milne:** "The End" from *Now We Are Six*, by A. A. Milne. Copyright
1927 by E. P. Dutton, renewed © 1955 by A. A. Milne. Used by permission of Dutton Children's Books,
a division of Penguin Books USA Inc. ★ **M. Meyerkort:** "A Verse for the Night Before the Birthday," by
M. Meyerkort, from *Festivals, Family and Food*, by Diana Carey and Judy Large, published by Hawthorn
Press [Hawthorn House, 1 Lansdown Lane, Lansdown, Stroud, Gloucestershire, GL5 IBJ, distributed in
North America by Anthroposophic Press, Box 94A1, Hudson, NY 12534]. ★ **Charlotte Pomerantz:** "All
Asleep" from *All Asleep*, copyright © 1984 by Charlotte Pomerantz, reprinted by permission of Greenwillow,
a division of William Morrow & Company Inc. ★ **Clyde Watson:** "All Tucked In & Roasty Toasty," by
Clyde Watson, reprinted by permission of Philomel Books from *Catch Me and Kiss Me and Say It Again*,
copyright © 1978 by Clyde Watson. ★ **Nancy Willard:** "The Wise Cow Enjoys a Cloud" from *A Visit to
William Blake's Inn*, copyright © 1981 by Nancy Willard, reprinted by permission of Harcourt Brace &
Company. ★ **William Carlos Williams:** "Poem," by William Carlos Williams, from *Collected Poems of
William Carlos Williams, 1909–1939 vol. 1*. Copyright 1938 by New Directions Publishing Company.
Reprinted by permission. ★ **Jane Yolen:** "Grandpa Bear's Lullaby" from *Dragon Night and Other Lullabies*,
copyright © 1980 by Jane Yolen, reprinted by permission of Curtis Brown Ltd.

Library of Congress Cataloging-in-Publication Data
Dyer, Jane.
  Animal Crackers : a delectable collection of pictures, poems, and lullabies
for the very young / Jane Dyer. — 1st ed.
      p.   cm.
  Summary: An illustrated collection of Mother Goose rhymes, lullabies,
and contemporary verses that celebrate special times in a child's first years.
    ISBN 0-316-19766-1
    1. Children's poetry. 2. Lullabies. [1. Poetry — Collections.
  2. Nursery rhymes. 3. Lullabies.] I. Title.
  PN6109.97.D94   1996
  808.81'0083'3 — dc20   93-4244

10 9 8 7 6 5 4 3 2 1

IM

Published simultaneously in Canada by Little, Brown & Company (Canada) Limited

Paintings done in watercolors on Waterford 140-pound hot pressed paper.

Text set in Cochin by Typographic House and display type hand-drawn by the artist,
based on the typeface BeLucian.

Printed in Singapore